Penguin's Big Surprise

Originally titled
Pugwug and Little

Susie Jenkin-Pearce

Tina Macnaughton

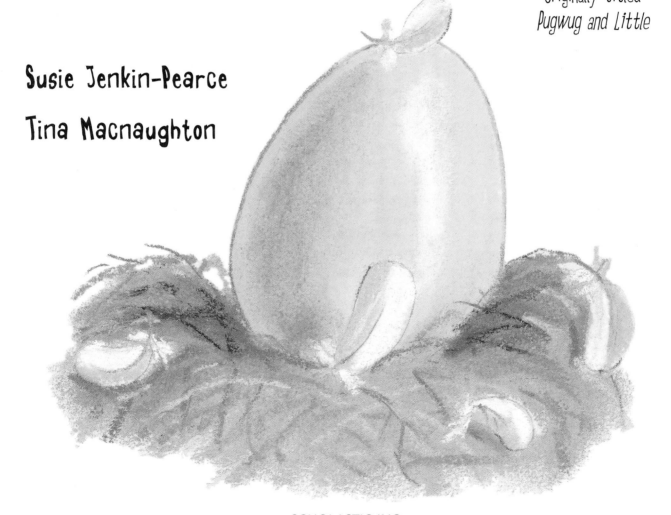

SCHOLASTIC INC.

New York   Toronto   London   Auckland   Sydney
Mexico City   New Delhi   Hong Kong   Buenos Aires

Pugwug was out slipping and sliding, when BANG, he bumped into something BIG.

Penguin's Big Surprise

Originally titled
Pugwug and Little

To my very dear friend Neil Mountain, with love
S.J-P.

To my mother, Ella Macnaughton
T.M.

Originally titled *Pugwug and Little*
No part of this publication may be reproduced, stored in a retrieval system,
or transmitted in any form or by any means, electronic, mechanical,
photocopying, recording, or otherwise, without written permission of the
publisher. For information regarding permission, write to School Specialty
Publishing, 8720 Orion Place, Columbus, OH 43240-2111.

ISBN-13: 978-0-439-02719-9
ISBN-10: 0-439-02719-5

12 11 10 9 8 7 6 5 4 3 2   7 8 9 10 11 12/0

Printed in the U.S.A.   40

First Scholastic printing, January 2007

Pugwug just had to know what
all the penguins were looking at.

He bounced . . .

He flapped . . .

He tried diving through a tiny gap . . .

. . . but it was no use.

Eventually, Big Penguin turned around. On his feet there was something large and round.

"Pugwug," said Big Penguin, "meet your
new little brother . . . or maybe sister!"

Pugwug was beside himself.
He shrieked with delight.
"Come on, Little," he
yelled, "let's play!"

But Little did not seem to want to play.
In fact, Little did nothing at all.

Pugwug tried to make Little look
more like a brother . . . or sister!

But he made a bit of a mess.
So Big Penguin had to give Little a wash.

"Come on – let's race!" said Pugwug.

"Or . . . let's play catch!" said Pugwug.

"Maybe not . . ." said Big Penguin gently.

"I know! How about football?" said Pugwug.

Big Penguin
was exhausted!

Suddenly a shout went up.
"Danger – seal alert! Penguin in trouble!"

"Pugwug," said Big Penguin gravely,
"look after Little. WATCH, but don't TOUCH!"
Then Big Penguin flapped away as fast as he could.

Pugwug and Little were
all on their own.

Suddenly, Little began
to wobble . . .

and shake
and rock and roll . . .

Pugwug didn't know
what to do . . . !

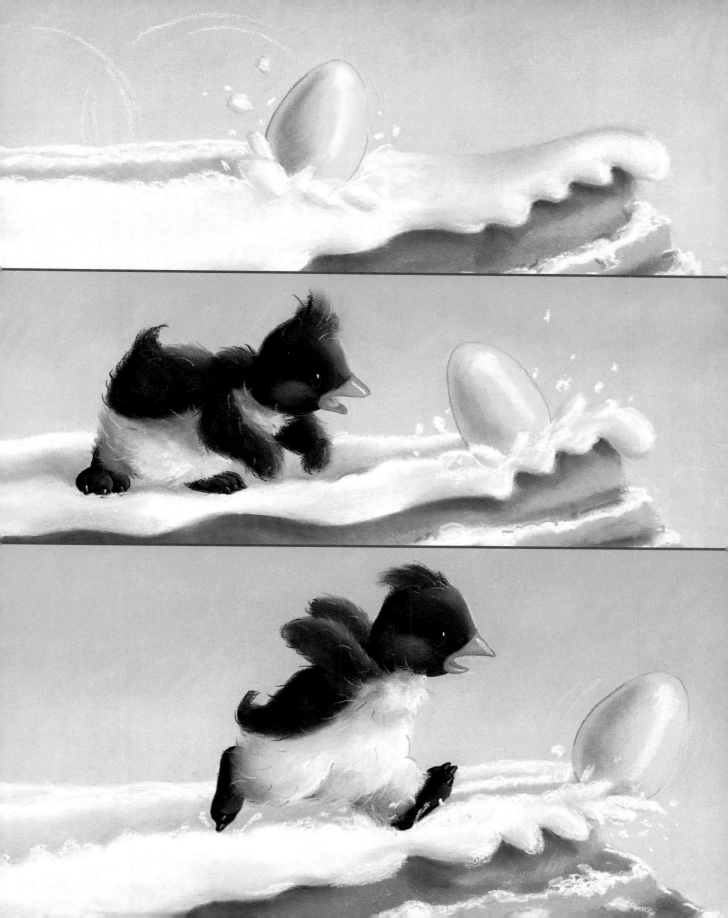

. . . but then he realized he HAD to touch!

Pugwug made
a great dive
and clasped Little
close to him.

When Big Penguin returned, he found
Little snuggled against Pugwug.
"Big Penguin," said Pugwug,
"meet my new baby . . .

. . . sister!"